WISE UP: GRANNIES ADVICES

Mind your character

First eBook Edition: June 2019

Artist: Paul Maposa

Design: E. Masundire

To the teacher/parent

Wise up: Grannies advices are short stories designed to equip school pupils with reading skills and to introduce them to the use of proverbs. The environment in which we grow in today does not promote the perpetual use of proverbs. These booklets therefore seek to hook the minds of children as they read them and instill the use of proverbs. They also provide a unique approach to the teaching of both reading and spelling for pupils.

Helping the child to learn reading is a gradual, repetitive and cumulative process which if not well handled may be a blow to the child's ego. The tireless reading needed to transform the child may be so cumbersome to the extent of driving him away from books. The **Wise up: Grannies advices** series however are designed to draw the children's attention to books. There are 14 booklets in this series providing a variety good enough to kill any sense of straying monotony. They provide well illustrated and interesting content. Besides being a source of entertainment, they also create and stimulate creativity in pupils thereby laying out a good foundation for creative writing and storytelling in children.

The children can use the books under the guidance of both the teacher at school and the parent at home. Involvement of the teacher and parent to the child's learning creates a supportive and encouraging atmosphere which is a necessity to every child. It is important for the teacher and parent to know that each book can be read many times by the learner. This strengthens the pupil's vocabulary as they go through each book.

Mind your character

This is Ben's father. Ben's father is a grown-up man. He is a good parent. He likes obedient children.

This is Ben's mother. She is a good farmer. She grows tomatoes and other vegetables for sale.

There is Ben and his father. Father want to send
Ben somewhere. Ben is an obedient child.

Ben helps his mother in the garden. He likes to help at home. He is a good obedient child.

Ben's mother always asks him to help. She wants him to carry a bucket of tomatoes. Ben always obeys his parents.

This is Mr. Jones. He is a visually impaired man. Mr. Jones does not see things around him. Mr. Jones always puts on black sunglasses.

Mr. Jones is seated by the wayside. Mr. Jones is begging for help. People always give him some money to help.

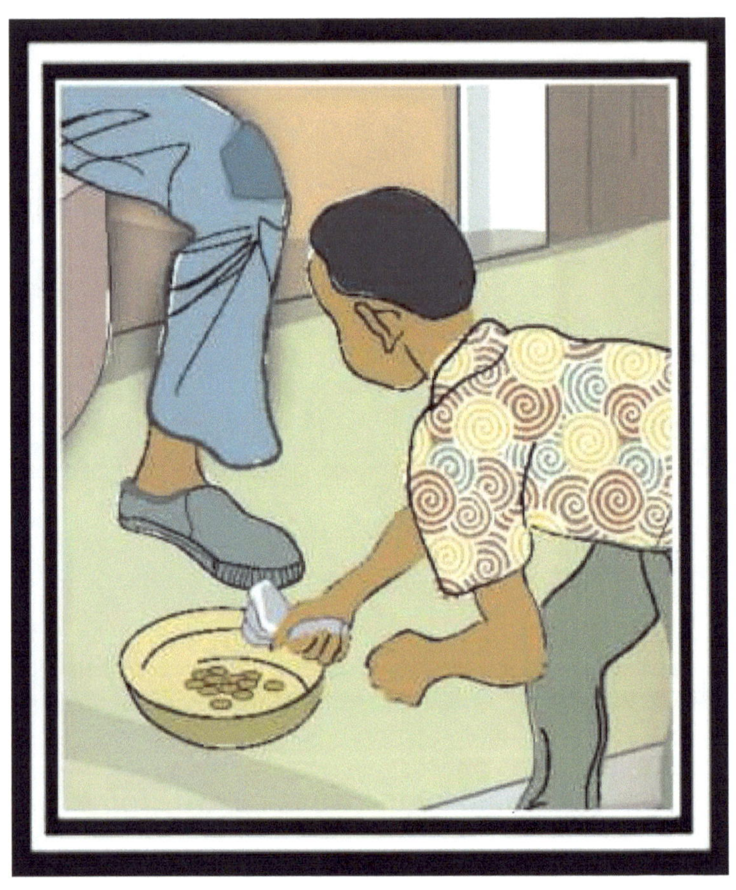

Ben saw Mr. Jones' money. He is taking away
Mr. Jones' money. Ben is stealing. Ben stole Mr.
Jones' money.

Ben is running away. He is running away with the stolen money. Stealing is bad. Ben is now a bad boy. All the good he did is gone.

Mind your character.

Read

1. obey
2. grow-up
3. parent
4. obedient
5. vegetables
6. sale
7. somewhere
8. garden
9. obey
10. impaired
11. always
12. sunglasses
13. visually
14. seated
15. people

16.money
17.wayside
18. begging
19.taking
20.stole
21.help
22.running
23. mind
24. character
25. Stealing

Complete these sentences

Impaired tomatoes stole obedient mother wayside

1. Ben's father likes ---- children.
2. Ben's ---- works in the garden.
3. They grow ---- in their garden
4. Mr. Jones is ----
5. He begs by the ----
6. Ben ---- from Mr. Jones.

Match the opposites

like	giving
good	later
man	walking
on	girl
seated	disobedient
begging	dislike
running	woman
boy	bad
now	off
obedient	standing

Make Words

1. st-
2. th-
3. wa-
4. bl-
5. ch

Make sentences:

1. father
2. parents
3. around
4. money
5. wayside
6. steal

Discuss

1. How do you make your parents happy?
2. What does the word steal mean?
3. What are the benefits of obedience?
4. How do you help your parents at home?
5. Why do we need to help at home?
6. Where do you find the disadvantaged in our community?
7. How do you tell that someone is blind?
8. How would you help a blind person in a busy area?
9. Besides giving money how do help the disadvantaged?
10. What should you do when you are tempted to steal?

Story telling

1. Tell a story on how you were so helpful to someone.
2. Imagine yourself at the hospital. Tell your friends a story of the disadvantaged people you saw.
3. Imagine yourself as Mr. Jones, tell your friends the problems you face and suggest how they can help you.

4. look at the picture and tell your friends a
   story on dangers of begging as a child.

Honesty and integrity

1. How do you make your parents trust you?
2. What sort of behaviors make children untrustworthy?
3. Why is it bad to tell a lie about someone else?
4. Why is it important to keep our promises?
5. Why is it dangerous to keep secrets about bad things you have done?

Chores training

1. Which duties should you do at home
    without help?

2. What do you like about your bedroom?
3. How do you make your bedroom always
    look tide?
4. Which of your home rules is difficulty for
    you to follow?
5. What are the most important chores you
    do at home?
6. Why are they important?

Life Application

1. Think of a kind gesture you can do at your school or in your community.
2. Write a story to encourage other children to help out at home and at school.

Training Techniques to the parent/guardian/teacher

Sharing and caring is a virtue that children can be trained to acquire. These virtues teach them about compromise and fairness. The following are tips on how to do it:

a) Start early to teach caring and sharing. This will train them to be generous, and be able to notice and respond to the needs of others as well as ability to meet their own needs.

b) Train them to control their egocentric impulses of grabbing everything for themselves and learn to let go and receive from others.

c) Train them delayed gratification through respecting the needs of others.

d) Give them the opportunity to experience the joy of giving through participation in family acts of kindness.

e) During training do not force them to give or to share. Rather train them to effectively communicate their needs for sharing and giving. Do not entertain crying as a way to communicate requests because its manipulative
f) Avoid labelling possessions as it creates competition and possessive behavior.
g) Praise them when they show effort to share and give.
h) Lead by example and ask them to hand out gifts you have prepared for others.